Zeus's Lovers

Welcome to the World of Mythology

Mythology gives you interesting explanations about life and satisfies your curiosity with stories that have been made up to explain surprising or frightening phenomena. People throughout the world have their own myths. In the imaginary world of mythology, humans can become birds or stars. The sun, wind, trees, and the rest of the natural world are full of gods who often interact with humans.

Greek and Roman mythology began more than 3,000 years ago. It consisted of stories first told by Greeks that lived on the shores of the Mediterranean Sea. In Italy the Romans would later borrow and modify many of these stories.

Most of the Greek myths were related to gods that resided upon the cloud-shrouded Mount Olympus. These clouds frequently could create a mysterious atmosphere on Mount Olympus. The ancient Greeks thought that their gods dwelt there and had human shapes, feelings, and behavior. The Greeks and the Romans built temples, offered animal sacrifices, said prayers, performed plays, and competed in sports to please their humanlike gods on Mount Olympus.

How did the world come into being in the first place?

Why is there night and day?

How did the four seasons come into existence?

Where do we go after we die?

Reading Greek and Roman mythology can help you understand ancient human ideas about our world. Since many Western ideas originated with the Greeks and Romans, you will benefit from taking a look into the mythology that helped to shape those important classical cultures. Understanding their mythology will give you an interesting view of the world you live in.

The characters in the stories

Zeus

He was accorded supreme authority to judge everything that occurred on Mount Olympus and on earth.
Zeus's many infidelities with beautiful goddesses and mortal women caused his wife Hera to be jealous.

Hera

She was the jealous wife of Zeus and the goddess of marriage. Hera was always suspicious of her promiscuous husband, Zeus. As a result, Zeus's many lovers suffered from Hera's acts of revenge.

Io

As one of the lovers of Zeus, Io was severely harassed by jealous Hera. Io gave birth to Zeus's son, Epaphus.
Her son later came to the throne of Egypt.

Callisto

She was a nymph of the forest and the best friend of the goddess of the hunt, Artemis. Tricked by Zeus' magic, Callisto had a son with Zeus named Arcas. This made Hera jealous, and Hera turned Callisto and Arcas into bears. Later, Callisto was transformed into a star constellation with Arcas.

Danae

She was a daughter of Acrisius, the king of Argos. Owing to the prophecy that one day her son would kill his grandfather, Acrisius, she was locked in a dungeon.

Alcmene

Alcmene was such a beautiful woman that she had many suitors. However, she became the wife of an ordinary man, Amphitryon. Disguised as her husband, Zeus visited Alcmene. She gave birth to Zeus's son, Hercules, who became a famous Greek hero.

Before Reading *the Zeus' Lovers*

The king of the gods, Zeus, and his wife, Hera, were a son and a daughter of Cronus and Rhea. Hera was an older sister of Zeus.

As soon as Hera was born, Cronus swallowed Hera. He did the same thing to his other children out of fear of the prophecy that he would lose his power to his children. However, the sixth child, Zeus, escaped from being devoured by his father, thanks to the wits of his mother, Rhea, and his grandmother, Gaea.

When Zeus reached maturity, he changed himself into a soaked, soggy cuckoo to win over Hera who didn't want to accept him. Finally, Zeus won Hera's sympathy, and they were married. Since Zeus had many licentious affairs with other goddesses and mortal women, he often had arguments with Hera. Finally, Hera's jealousy turned into dangerous revenge, putting Zeus and his lovers in trouble.

The book, Zeus's Lovers contains a few of the many love affairs of Zeus.

While Zeus was alone with Io, surprised by the sudden appearance of Hera, Zeus turned Io into a cow. In revenge, angry Hera set Argos and a gadfly to pester Io.

Tricked by Zeus, who loved her, Callisto ended up losing her best friend and her son, and finally she was transformed into a bear.

Danae had a son after Zeus approached her in the form of a golden rain shower. She and her son were unfairly thrown out to sea.

This is not everything. Don't forget Alcmene, who, because of Zeus, lost her brother and father. Alcmene and her husband were deserted on an isolated island. Hercules, the son of Zeus and Alcmene, is the main character in Hero Hercules, the fourth book in the series of Let's Enter the World of Mythology.

Let's take a closer look at some of the love stories of Zeus. Maybe these stories about Hera, Zeus, and Zeus's beautiful lovers can teach us how to avoid some trouble in our own lives.

Contents

Introduction

These stories are about Zeus, his wife,
and his lovers.

Zeus was the king of the gods. He was perfect
in many ways. But he had one problem.
He was always falling in love with beautiful
women! Of course, this made Hera very angry.

Hera was a good wife.

But she hated Zeus's lovers.

Hera could not tell Zeus what to do.

He was the king of the gods!

But Hera was smart.

She knew a way to keep women away from Zeus.

She would punish her husband's lovers.

Hera's punishments would be terrible!

Then other women would be afraid to be with Zeus.

Io

The cow was actually a beautiful
young woman named Io.

One day, Hera was relaxing in her
palace in the sky.

She noticed a cloud suddenly appear.

Its shadow hid a small part of the earth below.

Hera thought the cloud was strange.

So she pushed it away.

When the shadow moved, Hera could see
her husband. He was standing near a river.
Next to him was a beautiful cow.
Hera thought Zeus had changed a woman
into this cow.
He often changed his lovers into animals or
plants. He did this to hide them from Hera.

Hera was right. The cow was actually
a beautiful young woman named Io.
When Hera moved the cloud,
Zeus changed her into a cow.

Hera flew down to Zeus.

"My, what a lovely creature," said Hera.

"I've never seen such a beautiful cow.

Won't you give it to me as a gift?

I've never owned such a beautiful animal."

How could Zeus say no?

He knew his wife was smart.

So he gave her the cow.

He planned to get Io back later.

03

But Hera gave the cow to Argus.

Argus was a giant with one hundred eyes.

He could watch the cow all day and all night.

Even when Argus slept,

he kept two eyes open.

Argus put the cow in his field.

He always watched her closely.

At night, Argus tied a rope around Io's neck. She could not escape.
Io wanted to tell Argus who she was.
But when she opened her mouth, the only thing she could say was, "MoooOOOOO!"

One day, she saw her sisters and father walking nearby. She ran up to them.

The family was surprised to see such a beautiful cow.
Io tried to speak to them.
But all she could say was, "Moo!"
When her family started to leave, she blocked their way.
She needed to tell them who she was.

Suddenly, she had an idea.

She could write her name in the dirt!

With her front leg, she carefully wrote 'I-O' on the ground.

Her father threw his arms around her furry neck. And he began to cry.

"Oh, my darling daughter!" he cried.

"You are alive! But I cannot help you!"

Zeus saw everything from his throne.

He felt sorry for Io.

He called the god Hermes to him.

Hermes had wings on his feet and carried a magic wand. Hermes used the wand to make people sleepy.

"Go to Argus," Zeus told Hermes.

"Make him fall asleep. When he is asleep, bring me the beautiful cow."

Hermes flew down to the earth.

He took the wings off his feet and hid them.

He disguised himself as a shepherd.

Then he bought several sheep from a farmer.

Hermes now looked like a shepherd with
a flock of sheep!

He went to Argus's field.

Hermes pretended not to see Argus.

He started to play music on his flute.

Argus liked the sound of Hermes's music.

He spoke to Hermes.

"Shepherd, come sit by me."

Hermes sat by Argus and started to tell him a long and boring story.

Argus began to feel tired.

One by one, the giant's eyes closed.

At the end of the story, all of Argus's eyes were shut. He was snoring loudly!

Argus and Hermes

Hermes got up and walked over to Io.

But Hera was watching.

She flew down from the sky.

She was screaming in anger.

Hermes had no time to pick up Io.

He put his wings on his feet very,
very quickly.

Then he flew away even faster.

Hera was very angry at Argus for falling
asleep. She pulled out all of Argus's eyes!
Then she put them on the tail of a nearby
peacock. That is how the peacock got its
beautiful tail.

Hera was still angry.
She wanted to punish Io.
At that time, she saw a big fly that liked to
bite animals.

Hera put a spell on the fly.
The spell made the fly want
to bite Io again and again.
Io tried to run away
from the mad biting fly.
But the fly could follow
her easily.
Io ran and ran.
She jumped into the sea
and swam to the other side.

But the fly
continued to
bite her sides
and head.
Io went across
plains and climbed
mountains.
But the fly always
ran after her.

Io 21

Zeus saw how Hera had punished Io.

He felt pity for his lover.

He begged his wife to stop the fly.

He promised that he would never meet Io again.

He also promised to be a good husband.

Hera knew that he was sincere.

So Hera took her spell away from the fly.

It stopped chasing Io.

Then Zeus took his own
spell away from Io.
She turned into a young
woman again.
Slowly, she tried to speak.
She was afraid that she
would hear herself say, "Moo!"
But instead, she heard her own soft voice.
She was so happy that she ran back home,
singing.

Afterwards, Io never wanted another lover.
She would not even
look at men other
than her father.
She would only work
in her father's fields.
She would never
forget Hera's
punishment.

Callisto

Hera had turned Callisto
into a black bear!

A rtemis and Callisto were best friends.
Artemis was the goddess of the hunt.
Callisto was a wood nymph.
They enjoyed hunting and living in the
woods.

"Promise me one thing," said Artemis to
Callisto.

"Don't ever get married.

If you marry, you will run off to the city.

You will forget about me.

I would be very lonely without you."

"Don't worry," said Callisto,

"I have no interest in men.

I only care about living with you in the forest.

I promise I will never get married."

One day, Zeus saw Callisto who was hunting.
"I must meet that girl," said Zeus to himself.
"I've never seen a more beautiful girl!"
But Zeus knew that Callisto only cared
about Artemis.
'I must make myself look like Artemis,'
thought Zeus, 'then Callisto will trust me.'

First, Zeus changed his appearance to look
like Artemis.
Then, he went to Callisto.

"Ah, there you are," said Zeus.

"Come with me and eat lunch.

I have found some lovely grapes for us."

Callisto gladly ate the grapes.

Callisto didn't know Zeus had put a spell
on the grapes.

This spell would make her fall in love with
the first man or god she saw.

Zeus watched Callisto eating the first grape.

Suddenly, he changed back to his original appearance.

The spell worked.

Callisto fell in love with Zeus.

Callisto became Zeus's lover.

Callisto and Zeus

Now she had no time for Artemis.

Artemis became very angry at Callisto.

Artemis decided not to speak to Callisto again.

Zeus could not spend
all his time being with
Callisto.
Soon, he left
Callisto alone for
days and weeks.
Callisto became
lonely when Zeus
was gone.

One happy day, Callisto gave birth to a son.

'Now I will never be
alone,' she thought.
"What a beautiful
baby you are!
You look just like
your father, Zeus.
I will name you
'Arcas'."

 Callisto taught Arcas everything about the forest. Soon Arcas became strong and independent. When he was five years old, Arcas looked almost exactly like Zeus.

One day, Hera was walking through the forest. She saw Arcas. She was surprised. Arcas looked very familiar!

'That boy looks exactly like my husband,'
thought Hera.
'What has Zeus done?'

Hera became very angry.
She told Arcas to bring her to his mother.
Arcas pointed at Callisto, who was nearby.
"I'll teach you!" screamed Hera at Callisto.
"I'll take away the beauty that attracted
my husband!"
In seconds, Callisto saw big black hairs
growing from her skin.
Her fingernails
turned into claws.
When Callisto
screamed, she heard
the roar of a bear.
Hera had turned
Callisto into a black
bear!

Callisto ran to her son, Arcas.
But Arcas did not recognize her.
He thought a big black bear was attacking him!
Arcas turned and ran away.

He hid from his mother.
Arcas didn't know what happened to his mother.

 10

He spent years looking for her in the forest.
He was lonely.
But he knew how to live in the woods.
He grew up into a fine strong young man.

Callisto also wandered in
the forest.
She tried to find her son.
Every day she became
lonelier.
She felt very sorry for
herself.

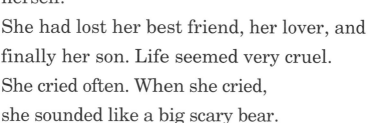

She had lost her best friend, her lover, and
finally her son. Life seemed very cruel.
She cried often. When she cried,
she sounded like a big scary bear.

One day Callisto
saw her son hunting.
She was so happy.
She wanted to greet her son.
Callisto stood up on her hind
legs. But when Arcas saw her,
he picked up his spear to kill the bear.

Luckily, Zeus was
watching everything.
He knew the bear was
Callisto.
He recognized Arcas as
his son.
Zeus did not want such a
terrible thing to happen.

Suddenly, Zeus grabbed Arcas and Callisto.
Then he threw both of them into the stars!
Callisto became the Great Bear and
Arcas became the Little Bear.
Even today, they are still shining among
the stars.

34

Danae

Zeus came again and again
to rain upon Danae.

A crisius was the king of Argos.
Danae was his daughter.
Danae grew up to be a beautiful young
princess.
But Acrisius was not happy.
He wanted a son who could become a king
when he died.

Acrisius went to the oracle at Delphi.
"Oracle, please tell me how I can have
a son," he said.
"I am getting old. I need someone to be
a king when I am gone."
The oracle gave Acrisius bad news.
"You will never have a son.

Instead, your
daughter will
have a son.
But your
grandson will
kill you."
Acrisius's face
grew white.
A member of
his own family
would kill him!

Acrisius was very afraid of death.

And he hated the idea of being killed by his own grandson!

'I know what I must do,' he thought.

'I must stop Danae from having a child.

If she never gives birth,

then I won't be killed.'

Acrisius called his servants to him.

"I want you to lock Danae in my prison.

I never want her to see the light of day again!"

The servants grabbed Danae.

She screamed as they put her in prison.

"Why are you doing this?" she screamed.

"What did I do to deserve this?"

Danae spent many years in prison.

She never saw daylight and never spoke to another person.

Danae became very sad and lonely.

But Zeus could see Danae.

He could see everything over, on, or below the ground.

'Someone so beautiful should never be lonely,' he thought.

'I will go to her and be her friend.'

But Zeus was worried.

'If I walked through the walls to see her, she would be afraid.

Instead, I will become the form of a golden rain. I will pour down onto Danae and make her happy!'

Golden Rain Falling Down on Danae

When Danae looked up at the ceiling,
she saw golden rain falling.
It was clean and beautiful.

Danae felt happy for the first time in prison.

She forgot all of her problems.

Zeus came again and again to rain upon Danae.

One day, he rained on her for many hours.

The golden water went through Danae's skin.

In the water was Zeus's seed.

 Danae became pregnant.

Her stomach grew large.

A guard noticed Danae's big stomach.

He went to King Acrisius.

"Oh, mighty King,

the princess will soon have a baby!"

Acrisius became very angry.

"How did this happen?" he screamed.

"You must have allowed a man to visit her!

All of you guards will be punished!"

The guards were killed.

New guards were put in the prison.

Danae remained locked in her cell.

Finally, Danae had a son.

She named him 'Perseus'.

Acrisius had Danae and Perseus brought to him.

"So this is the grandson who will kill me one day?" he said.

"Well, I will not permit it!

Guards! Put them in a wooden box!

Then throw the box into the sea!"

The guards did as the
king ordered.
But the box did not sink.
Instead, it floated on
the water.
The box was carried
far away by the waves.
Danae and Perseus
had no food or water.

After a long time, the
box came to the island
of Serifos.
The king of this island
was Dictys.
He watched the box
come in from the sea.
"Bring me that box,"
Dictys told his servants.

"Let's see what's inside."

King Dictys was shocked to see Danae and
Perseus.

"Please bring us something to eat and drink,"
cried Danae.

King Dictys was a kind man.

He gave them food and water.

And he told his servants to help them.

Soon Danae and Perseus were healthy
again.

Danae told King Dictys their story.
The king was horrified by Acrisius's
behavior.
How could a man be so mean to his own
family?

Dictys liked Danae.
She was a strong
woman and a good
mother.
She had protected
Perseus and kept him alive.
Danae had the beauty, grace, and charm of
a queen. So Dictys married Danae.

Perseus grew up to be a strong young man.
He had many adventures.
On one adventure,
he met Acrisius and killed him.
Then he became the king of Argos,
Acrisius's country.

Alcmene

A lcmene was another woman Zeus loved. Of course, she was very beautiful.

Many men were attracted to her.

But she was married to an ordinary man named Amphitryon.

People thought Amphitryon was very lucky to have Alcmene.

But Amphitryon's luck did not last.

Zeus soon noticed Alcmene.

He fell in love at first sight.

Zeus wanted to be alone with Alcmene.

But this would be difficult.

She was married and spent most of her
time with her husband.

Zeus would have to make a plan.

A few days later, Alcmene got some terrible news. Her brothers had been killed! The story went like this:

An old shepherd saw the brothers trying to steal sheep. He scared them away.
But the old man knew the brothers would come back. So he brought his four sons to the field.
He told his sons to hide and wait.
When Alcmene's brothers returned, the sons killed them all.

16

When Alcmene heard this story, she did
not cry. Instead, she became very angry.

"Why should my brothers be punished so
badly? Their crime was not so serious.
They should have gone to prison.
They should not have been killed."

Alcmene talked to her husband.

"I demand revenge. Their killer is an old
shepherd. He lives on the other side of this
island. Please, kill him."

But Amphitryon didn't want to do this.

Alcmene would ask him again and again
to kill the old shepherd.
Amphitryon had no peace.
He knew his wife would never
forgive the shepherd.
So he went to the other side
of the island.

He climbed the highest
hill he could find.
Then he looked for sheep.
He saw a large flock.

There was an old man
with the sheep.
Amphitryon came down
from the hill.
He hid in some bushes and
fell asleep.

50

At night, Amphitryon woke up. He went to
the field where he saw the old man.

A few hours later, he saw an old man walking.
The night was very dark.
Therefore Amphitryon could not see the
man's face.
'It must be the old shepherd,'
thought Amphitryon.
He waited until the old man was close.
Then he jumped up and pushed his knife
into the man's back. The old man died.

Amphitryon returned home.

But his wife was crying.

"Alcmene, why are you crying?" he asked.

"Oh! Someone has killed my father,"
cried Alcmene.

"Father was walking back to his house
late at night. Someone must have thought
he was a thief!"

Alcmene held her face in her hands.

"Oh, this is terrible," she cried.

"I have lost my brothers and my father
in one week! I can't stand it!"

Amphitryon then realized that he had
killed his wife's father.

He felt terrible.

He decided to tell his wife the truth.

"Please forgive me, dear wife," he said.

"I killed your father.

I thought he was the old shepherd.

Please forgive me!"

Alcmene fell to the floor.

"This is the worst thing that could happen!"
she said. "How can this be true?"

Amphitryon walked outside.

There were many people in the street.

"I killed my wife's father," he shouted.

"Please decide my punishment.

I must pay for my mistake."

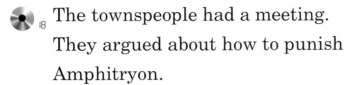 The townspeople had a meeting.

They argued about how to punish
Amphitryon.

Finally, they decided to send him to a
small island nearby. No one lived on that
island. Amphitryon could not hurt anyone
there.

Alcmene began to cry again.

She was angry that her husband had killed

her father. But she knew it was a mistake.

"I must forgive my husband,"

she told the townspeople.

"When I married him,

I agreed to stay with him forever.

I will go with him to the island."

So both Amphitryon and Alcmene left their

town.

Amphitryon was happy that his wife went

with him. But she was still angry with him.

On the first day on the small island,
Alcmene spoke to Amphitryon.
"I still want revenge for my brothers,"
she said.
"I will not speak to you again until
you have killed the shepherd."

Amphitryon was upset because he could
not talk with his wife.
Finally, he could not stand it any longer.
He packed his weapons and left the small
island.

Amphitryon was not
supposed to be on the
shepherd's island.
So he had to be careful.
He only traveled at
night and he slept in
the hills.

He traveled slowly.
He didn't want anyone to see him.

He was gone
from his wife
for several
months.
Amphitryon
started to miss
Alcmene very
much.

This was the perfect chance for Zeus.
Actually, Zeus had created this entire
situation.

Zeus made sure that Alcmene's brothers
were killed.

He caused Alcmene to demand revenge.

And he made the townspeople send
Amphitryon and his wife to the deserted
island.

Now Zeus could be
alone with Alcmene.
His plan was
successful.
Zeus flew to the
small island.
He changed his
appearance.

He now looked like Amphitryon.

Zeus went to Alcmene and said,
"I have returned, my wife.
I have killed the old shepherd.
You have your revenge."
Alcmene dropped her basket and ran to
Zeus. She hugged and kissed him.
"Dearest Amphitryon!
You have done what I asked!
You really love me!
Now I can love you again with all my heart."
Alcmene did not know that she was actually
speaking to Zeus.

One day, Zeus knew
Amphitryon was
coming back to the
island.
So he left before
husband and wife
saw each other.

Amphitryon went
to Alcmene.
He bent down on
his knee.
"I am so sorry, dear
Alcmene. I was not
able to kill the
shepherd.

When I saw his old face, I felt pity for him.
I just could not kill him.
Please, forgive me!"

Alcmene was confused. "What are you talking about? You said you killed him eight months ago!

Come inside, dear. I think you've been in the sun too long."

Amphitryon didn't know what was going on.

He never did understand what Alcmene had meant that day.
But he decided not to talk about it again.
In the same way, Alcmene never knew that Zeus had loved her.

For Amphitryon, his wife was the most forgiving person in the world.
For Alcmene, her husband was the greatest hero ever.

Reading Comprehension

Read and answer the questions.

▶ **Io**

1. What did Zeus change Io into?

    (A) a monster
    (B) a goddess
    (C) a gift
    (D) a cow

2. Why was Io unable to speak to her family?

    (A) Because she could only say "Moo!"
    (B) Because she was always eating.
    (C) Because she had been turned into a fly.
    (D) Because she was crying too hard to speak.

3. How did Hera punish Io?

    (A) She picked the eyes out of Io's head.
    (B) She sent a fly to bite Io.
    (C) She decorated a peacock with Io's eyes.
    (D) She hit Io's head.

▶ **Callisto**

4. What did the magic grapes do to Callisto?

   (A) They made her fall in love with Artemis.

   (B) They made her lose all interest in men.

   (C) They made her hate Artemis.

   (D) They made her fall in love with Zeus.

5. What did Hera do to Callisto?

   (A) She turned Callisto into a bear.

   (B) She turned Callisto into a strong young man.

   (C) She threw Callisto into the stars.

   (D) She scolded Callisto soundly.

6. How did Zeus prevent Arcas from killing Callisto?

   (A) He made them disappear.

   (B) He took away Arcas's spear.

   (C) He threw Arcas and Callisto into the stars.

   (D) He told Arcas not to.

7. Why did Acrisius want a son?

   (A) Because he hated his daughter.
   (B) Because he wanted a son to become a king
       after he died.
   (C) Because sons are stronger than daughters.
   (D) Because he was a coward.

8. Why did Acrisius have Danae locked up
   in prison?

   (A) So that she would never have a son.
   (B) Because he hated her.
   (C) So that she wouldn't kill Acrisius.
   (D) Because it was good for her health.

9. What happened when the guards threw the box
   into the sea?

   (A) It sunk.
   (B) It broke.
   (C) It bounced.
   (D) It floated.

▸ Alcmene

10. Why was Amphitryon a lucky man?

    (A) Because he was a king.

    (B) Because he had a beautiful wife.

    (C) Because he was a rich man.

    (D) Because he was a handsome man.

11. Why was Alcmene's father killed?

    (A) Because Amphitryon mistook him for an old shepherd.

    (B) Because Alcmene stole sheep.

    (C) Because Amphitryon was an evil man.

    (D) Because Alcmene's father was an old man.

12. Why did Zeus have Alcmene's brothers killed?

    (A) Because he hated them.

    (B) Because he liked sad stories.

    (C) Because he enjoyed tricking Alcmene.

    (D) Because he wanted to be alone with Alcmene.

● Read and talk about it.

> . . . Afterwards, Io never wanted another lover.
> She would not even look at men other than her father.
> She would only work in her father's fields.
> She would never forget Hera's punishment.

1. What's the meaning of 'She would never forget Hera's punishment.'?
   What would you have done if you were Io?

> . . . One day Callisto saw her son as he was hunting.
> She was so happy. She wanted to greet her son.
> Callisto stood up on her hind legs.
> But when Arcas saw her, he picked up his spear to kill the bear. . . .

2. In this situation, what would you have done if you were Callisto?

> . . . 'I know what I must do,' he thought.
> 'I must stop Danae from having a child.
> If she never gives birth, then I won't be killed.'
> Acrisius called his servants to him.
> "I want you to lock Danae in my prison.
> I never want her to see the light of day again!". . .

3. Acrisius locked Danae in his prison. But wasn't there another way for him to deal with his daughter? What would you have done if you were Acrisius ?

> . . . The night was very dark.
> Therefore Amphitryon could not see the man's face.
> 'It must be the old shepherd,' thought Amphitryon.
> He waited until the old man was close.
> Then he jumped up and pushed his knife into the man's back. The old man died. . . .

4. Amphitryon thought that Alcmene's father was the old shepherd. In this situation, what would you have done if you were Amphitryon?

The Signs of the Zodiac

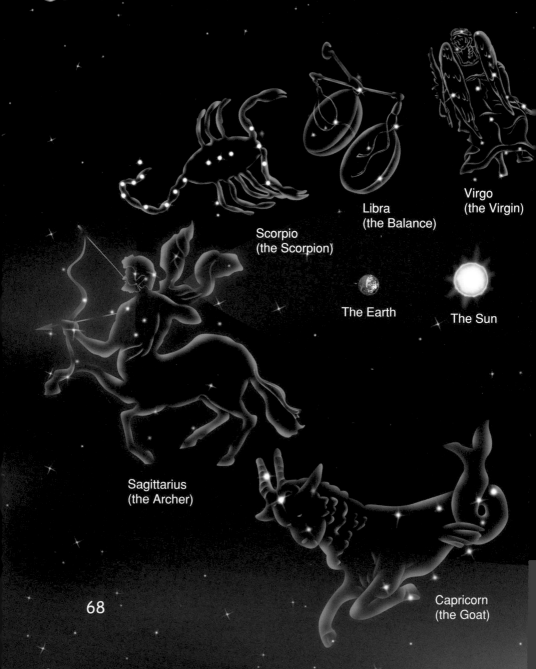

21

Scorpio
(the Scorpion)

Libra
(the Balance)

Virgo
(the Virgin)

The Earth

The Sun

Sagittarius
(the Archer)

Capricorn
(the Goat)

The word 'zodiac' comes from a Greek word meaning, "the circle of animals". Where did the zodiac come from? In this section, you can find the Greek Myths that explain the origins of these signs.

Leo
(the Lion)

Cancer
(the Crab)

Gemini
(the Twins)

Taurus
(the Bull)

Aquarius
(the Water Bearer)

Pisces
(the Fishes)

Aries
(the Ram)

69

22

Aries (the Ram)

March 21st ~ April 20th

The origin of Aries stems from the Tale of the Golden Ram. The ram safely carried off Phrixus.

Phrixus sacrificed the Golden Ram to Zeus and in turn, Zeus placed the ram in the heavens.

Taurus (the Bull)

April 21st ~ May 20th

The origin of Taurus stems from the Tale of Europa and the Bull. Zeus turned himself into a bull in order to attract Europa to him.

The bull carried Europa across the sea to Crete.

In remembrance, Zeus placed the image of the bull in the stars.

Gemini (the Twins)

May 21st ~ June 21st

This sign stems from the Tale of Castor and Pollux. Castor and Pollux were twins. They both loved each other very much. In honor of the brothers's great love, Zeus placed them among the stars.

 23

Cancer (the Crab)

June 22nd ~ July 22nd

The sign of Cancer stems from one of the 12 Labors of Hercules.

Hera sent the crab to kill Hercules. But Hercules crushed the crab under his foot just before he defeated the Hydra. To honor the crab, Hera placed it among the stars.

Leo (the Lion)
July 23rd ~ August 22nd

The sign of Leo stems from another of Hercules 12 Labors. Hercules's first labor was to kill a lion that lived in Nemea valley. He killed the Nemea lion with his hands. In remembrance of the grand battle, Zeus placed the Lion of Nemea among the stars.

Libra (the Balance)
September 23rd ~ October 21st

The Libra are the scales that balance justice. They are held by the goddess of divine justice, Themis. Libra shines right beside Virgo which represents Astraea, daughter of Themis.

Virgo (the Virgin)
August 23rd · September 22nd

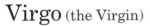

Virgo's origin stems from the Tale of Pandora. Virgo represents the goddess of purity and innocence, Astraea. After Pandora opened the forbidden box and let loose all the evils into the world, every god went back to heaven. As a remembrance of innocence lost, Astraea was placed amongst the stars in the form of Virgo.

Scorpio (the Scorpion)
October 22nd ~ November 21st

The sign of Scorpio stems from the Tale of Orion. Orion and Artemis were great hunting partners, which made Artemis's brother Apollo very jealous. Apollo pleaded with Gaea to kill Orion. So Gaea created the scorpion and killed great Orion. In remembrance of this act, Zeus placed Orion and the scorpion amongst the stars. But they never appear at the same time.

Sagittarius (the Archer)

November 23 rd ~ December 21 st

This sign is representative of Cheiron. Cheiron was the friend of many great heroes in Greek mythology such as Achilles and Hercules. Hercules accidentally shot Cheiron in the leg with a poison arrow. Cheiron was immortal so he couldn't die. Instead, he had to endure the unending pain. Cheiron begged Zeus to kill him. To honor Cheiron, Zeus placed him among the stars.

 25

Capricorn (the Goat)

December 22 nd ~ January 19 th

The sign of Capricorn represents the goat Amalthea who fed the infant Zeus. It's said that Zeus placed her among the stars in gratitude.

Aquarius
(the Water Bearer)

January 20 th ~ February 18 th

The sign of Aquarius stems from the Tale of Deucalion's Flood. In this tale, Zeus pours all the waters of the heavens onto earth to wash away all the evil creatures. Deucalion and his wife Pyrrha were the only survivors of the great flood.

Pisces (the Fishes)

February 19 th ~ March 20 th

The Pisces represents the goddess of love & beauty, Aphrodite and her son the god of love, Eros. They were taking a stroll down the Euphrates River when there was a typhoon. They pleaded for Zeus to help them escape, so Zeus changed them into fish and they swam away safely. In remembrance of this, Aphrodite is the big fish constellation and Eros is the small fish constellation.

希臘羅馬神話故事 **9**

宙斯的眾情人 Zeus's Lovers

First Published May, 2011
First Printing May, 2011

Original Story by Thomas Bulfinch
Rewritten by David O'Flaherty
Illustrated by Koltsova Irina
Designer by Eunjiu Park, Eonju No
Translated by Jia-chen Chuo

Printed and distributed by Cosmos Culture Ltd.
Tel: 02-2365-9739
Fax: 02-2365-9835
http://www.icosmos.com.tw
Publisher: Value-Deliver Culture Ltd.

Zeus's Lovers

中譯解答本

卓加真　譯

神話以趣味的方式，為我們生活中的煩惱提出解釋，並滿足我們的好奇心。許多故事的編寫，都是為了解釋一些令人驚奇或恐懼的現象，因此，世界各地不同的國家、民族，都有屬於自己的神話。

希臘與羅馬神話充滿想像力，並結合了諸神與英雄們激盪人心的傳奇故事，因此特別為人所津津樂道。希臘與羅馬神話反應了真實的人類世界，因此，閱讀神話對於瞭解西方文化與思維，有極大的幫助。

這些經典故事的背景，可追溯至史前時代，但對於當代的讀者而言，它們深具魅力的法寶何在？其秘密就在於，神話能超越時空，完整地呈現人類心中的慾望。這些激盪人心的冒險故事，將帶您經歷生命中的各種重要事件：戰爭與和平、生命與死亡、善與惡，以及各種愛恨情仇。

希臘與羅馬神話裡所描繪的諸神，並不全是完美、萬能的天神，他們和人類一樣，會因憤怒而打鬥，會耍詭計戲弄其他天神，會因愛與嫉妒而感到痛苦。在 Let's Enjoy Mythology 系列的第二部 Reading Greek and Roman Mythology in English 中，你將會讀到許多具有人類特質的英雄、女英雄、眾神和女神的故事。

Reading Greek and Roman Mythology in English 將引領你穿越時空，一探想像中的古希臘世界。

　　眾神之王宙斯和他的妻子赫拉,是克羅納斯與莉亞的子女,赫拉原是宙斯的姊姊。

　　因為曾有人預言,克羅納斯的兒女將奪走他的權力,因此赫拉一出生,克羅納斯便把她給吞了,對其他孩子亦然。不過克羅納斯的第六個孩子宙斯,卻因母親莉亞與祖母蓋亞的機智,而逃過一劫。

　　宙斯成年之後,赫拉不願接受他的追求,於是他化身為一隻濕淋淋的布穀鳥,想贏得她的芳心。最終,宙斯終於博得赫拉的同情,兩人結為夫妻。但是宙斯跟其他女神和凡女又有一堆風流債,兩人經常為此爭執不休。赫拉的嫉妒心終於演變成危險的報復行為,宙斯和他的愛人們麻煩大了。

　　《宙斯的眾情人》這本書,包含了宙斯諸多愛情故事裡的其中幾則。

　　當宙斯正與愛歐獨處之際,赫拉突然出現,驚嚇之餘,宙斯趕緊將愛歐變成了一頭乳牛。憤怒的赫拉為了報復,便派阿古士和一隻牛虻去騷擾愛歐。

　　卡麗絲托被愛她的宙斯所騙,結果失去了最要好的朋友和兒子,最後還被變成了一隻熊。

　　宙斯化身為金色雨水,淋在達妮身上,讓達妮生下了一個兒子。後來達妮和他的兒子受到不公平的待遇,被扔到海裡去了。

　　這還不是全部的故事,別忘了還有愛克美娜,也因為宙斯之故,失去了兄弟和父親,愛克美娜與其丈夫並離群住到荒島之上。宙斯與愛克美娜之子海克力斯,則是本系列中,第四冊《大力士海克力斯》的主角。

　　我們就來仔細讀一讀幾則宙斯的愛情故事吧,或許我們能從宙斯、赫拉和其情婦們的故事中,學會如何解決生活中的疑難雜症呢。

目錄

故事介紹

 p. 8

這些都是宙斯和妻子
及情婦之間的故事。
宙斯是眾神之王,
他在許多方面都是個完美的神祇,
但他有個毛病,
就是老愛上美麗的女子!
當然,這點讓赫拉很生氣。

- **lover** [ˈlʌvə(r)]
  情人;愛人
- **perfect** [ˈpɜːrfɪkt]
  完美的;理想的
- **in many ways** [ɪn meni weɪs] 在各方面
- **problem** [ˈprɑːbləm] 問題
- **was falling n love with**
  [wəz ˈfɔːlɪŋ ɪn lʌv wɪθ]
  愛上……
- **of course** [əv kɔːrs] 當然
- **made . . . angry**
  [meɪd ˈæŋgri] 使……生氣
  (made是make的過去式)

 p. 9

赫拉是個賢內助,
但她痛恨宙斯的情婦。
對此,赫拉無權置喙,
畢竟宙斯是眾神之王!
不過赫拉很精明,
她知道如何讓女子遠離宙斯,
她會懲罰宙斯的情婦。
她的懲罰,是非常可怕的!
以至於其他的女人
都不敢和宙斯在一起。

- **wife** [waɪf] 妻子
- **hate** [heɪt] 憎恨
- **smart** [smɑːrt] 聰明的
- **keep A away from B**
  使 A 遠離 B
- **punish** [ˈpʌnɪʃ]
  懲罰;使痛苦
- **punishment** [ˈpʌnɪʃmənt]
  懲罰
- **terrible** [ˈterəbl] 糟糕的
- **be afraid to** [bi əˈfreɪd tə]
  害怕去……

愛歐
乳牛

原來是一位名叫愛歐的美麗少婦。

p. 10

有一天，赫拉在天上的宮殿中休憩。
她注意到一朵雲突然出現，
雲朵遮住了一片陸地。
赫拉覺得事有蹊蹺，
就將雲朵驅散開來。

* **relax** [rɪˋlæks] 放鬆
* **palace** [ˋpæləs] 宮殿
* **notice** [ˋnoʊtɪs] 注意
* **suddenly** [ˋsʌdənli] 突然地
* **appear** [əˋpɪr] 出現
* **shadow** [ˋʃædoʊ] 影子
* **hide** [haɪd] 隱藏
* **a part of** ……的一部份
* **below** [bɪˋloʊ] 在下方
* **push . . . away**
  把……推開

p. 11

雲朵移開之後，
赫拉看到自己的丈夫。
丈夫站在河邊，
旁邊跟著一頭美麗的乳牛。
赫拉心想
宙斯又把哪個女子變成乳牛了，
他常常把情婦變成動物或植物，
以掩赫拉之耳目。

赫拉猜得沒錯；
這隻乳牛
其實是一位叫做愛歐的美麗少婦。
就在赫拉將雲朵驅散之時，
宙斯把她變成了一頭乳牛。

* **move** [mu.v] 移開
* **was standing**
  正站立於
* **near** [nɪə(r)] 附近；旁邊
* **next to** [nekst tə]
  緊鄰在……的旁邊
* **cow** [kaʊ] 母牛；乳牛
* **change A into B**
  [tʃeɪndʒ eɪ ɪntə bi]
  把 A 變成 B
* **animal** [ˋænɪml] 動物
* **plant** [plænt] 植物
* **actually** [ˋæktʃuəli]
  事實上；實際上

5

p. 12

赫拉飛向宙斯，說道：
「哇，這真是一隻可愛的動物，
我從沒見過這麼漂亮的牛。
你不把牠送給我當作禮物嗎？
我還不曾擁有過這麼美麗的動物呢。」

宙斯如何能拒絕請求呢？
他知道赫拉很精明，
只好把牛送給了她，
打算晚一點再把愛歐變回人。

- **flew** [flu:] 飛行
  （fly的過去式）
- **creature** [ˈkri:tʃə(r)]
  生物；不同於人的動物
- **never** [ˈnevə(r)]
  從沒有；未曾
- **seen** [si:n] 見到；看過
  （see的過去分詞）
- **such** [sʌtʃ] 如此……；
  這樣的……
- **as** [əz] 如……一般
- **own** [oʊn] 擁有
- **plan** [plæn] 計畫；打算

---

p. 13

然而，赫拉卻將乳牛交給了阿古士。
阿古士是一隻百眼巨怪，
可以日夜看守乳牛。
阿古士就算睡著了，
仍會有兩隻眼睛是張開著的。
他將乳牛放牧在自己的田園上，
嚴加看管。

- **Argus** [ˈɑrgəs] 阿古士
  （希神）（百眼巨人）
- **giant** [ˈdʒaɪənt] 巨大的
- **hundred** [ˈhʌndrəd]
  上百的
- **watch** [wɑ:tʃ] 看守
- **even** [i:vn] 即使……
- **slept** [slɛpt] 已睡著
  （sleep的過去式）
- **field** [fi:ld] 野地
- **closely** [ˈkloʊsli]
  緊緊地；靠近地

p. 14

夜裡,阿古士將繩索套在愛歐頸上,
以防她逃走。
愛歐想說明自己的身分,
但她一開口,
就只能發出「哞」的聲音!

這天,
她見到自己的父親和姊妹在附近散步,
便迅速跑向他們。

家人見到美麗的乳牛,很驚喜。
愛歐想對他們說話,
卻也只能發出「哞」的聲音。
就在家人要離去之時,
乳牛擋住了他們的去路。
她必須告訴家人自己的身分。

- **tied a rope around**
  [taɪd ə roʊp ə`raʊnd]
  綁了一根繩索在……
- **neck** [nek] 脖子
- **escape** [ə`skeɪp] 逃脫
- **nearby** [nɪəbaɪ] 在附近
- **surprised** [sə`praɪzd]
  驚訝的（surprise的過去
  式）
- **block** [blɑːk]
  阻礙;妨礙
- **need** [niːd] 需要;必要

7

p. 15

突然，她想了一個辦法，
她可以在地上寫自己的名字！
乳牛以自己的前蹄，
小心翼翼在地上寫著「愛──歐」。
父親張開雙臂，
擁抱著她毛茸茸的頸項，哭了起來。
「我親愛的女兒！」他哭著說：
「原來妳還活著，
可是我卻幫不上忙！」

- **idea** [aɪˋdiːə] 主意；想法
- **dirt** [dɜːt] 土；土壤
- **front** [frʌnt] 前面的
- **carefully** [ˋkerfəli]
  仔細的；小心的
- **ground** [graʊnd] 地上
- **furry** [ˋfɜːri] 毛皮覆蓋的
- **alive** [əˋlaɪv]
  在世的；活著的

---

p. 16

宙斯從寶座上看到了這一切，
他為愛歐感到很難過。
他召喚信差神荷米斯前來。
荷米斯的腳上長有一雙翅膀，
手中握著一根魔棒，
他可以用魔棒讓人們睡著。
宙斯告訴荷米斯：
「去找阿古士，讓他睡著，
待他熟睡之際，
把美麗的乳牛帶回來給我。」

- **throne** [θroʊn] 帝王寶座
- **felt sorry for**
  [felt ˋsɑːri fə(r)]
  為……感到難過的；為
  ……感到過意不去的
- **Hermes** 荷米斯（希神）
  （眾神的使者）
- **wing** [wɪn] 翅膀；翼
- **carried** [ˋkæri] 帶著
- **magic wand**
  [ˋmædʒɪk wɑːnd]
  神奇魔杖
- **asleep** [əˋsliːp] 睡著地
- **bring** [brɪŋ] 帶來；取來

p. 17

荷米斯飛到人間。
他將腳上的翅膀取下，藏起來，
並打扮成牧羊人的模樣，
然後從農夫那買來一些羊隻。
現在，荷米斯擁有一群羊，
十足像個牧羊人。

他來到阿古士的田園中，
假裝沒有看到他，
然後開始吹奏著笛子。

- **disguise** [dɪsˋgaɪz]
  假扮；偽裝
- **shepherd** [ˋʃɛpərd]
  牧羊人
- **several** [ˋsɛvrəl]
  多個的；數個的
- **bought** [bɔːt]
  購買（buy的過去式）
- **farmer** [ˋfɑːrmə(r)]
  農夫；農民
- **a flock of** [ə flɑːk əv]
  一群……
- **pretend to** [prɪˋtɛnd tə]
  假裝去……
- **flute** [fluːt] 笛子

p. 18

阿古士很喜歡荷米斯所吹的音樂，
他對荷米斯說：
「牧羊人，來坐在我身邊。」
荷米斯便坐在阿古士身邊，
對他說起一個又長又無聊的故事。
阿古士開始覺得疲累，
他巨大的眼睛，
就一個一個地闔上了。
等故事一說完，
阿古士的眼睛也都閉上了，
開始大聲打起呼來！
〔圖〕阿古士和荷米斯

- **spoke** [spoʊk] 交談；說話（speak的過去式）
- **sat down** [sæt daʊn] 坐下（sat是sit的過去式）
- **boring** [ˋbɔːrɪŋ] 無聊的；乏味的
- **one by one** [wʌn baɪ wʌn] 一個接著一個的
- **at the end of** [æt ði end ɑːv] 在……的最後
- **shut** [ʃʌt] 閉上了的
- **snore** [ˋsnɔː(r)] 打鼾
- **loudly** [ˋlaʊdli] 大聲地；高聲地

p. 19

荷米斯起身走到愛歐身邊，
但赫拉正監視著。
赫拉從天上飛下來，
怒斥荷米斯的行徑。
荷米斯沒來得及帶走愛歐，
他火速將翅膀裝上雙腳，
以更飛快的速度溜走了。

- **scream** [skiːm]（痛苦的）尖叫聲
- **in anger** [ɪn ˋæŋɡə(r)] 忿怒的；氣憤
- **had no time to** 沒有時間去……（had是have的過去式）
- **pick up** [pɪk ʌp] 救起
- **put** [pʊt] 放置
- **faster** [ˋfæstə(r)] 更快的（fast迅速的；fastest最迅速的）

p. 20

赫拉很生氣阿古士竟然睡著，
便將他的眼睛全部拔走，
然後放在附近一隻孔雀的尾巴上，
而這就是爲什麼
孔雀有著美麗尾巴的由來。

赫拉怒氣難消，
她想要懲罰愛歐。
當下，
她看到一隻喜歡叮咬動物的大蒼蠅。

- **fall asleep** [fɔ:l `əslip]
  進入睡眠狀態
- **pull out** [pʊl aʊt]
  拉出；取出
- **nearby** [`nɪəbaɪ] 在附近
- **peacock** [`pi:kɑ:k] 孔雀
  （尤指雄孔雀）
- **fly** [flaɪ] 蒼蠅
- **bite** [baɪt] 叮；咬

---

p. 21

赫拉對蒼蠅施加魔法，
讓蒼蠅直對著愛歐叮咬個不停。
愛歐努力想擺脫這隻煩人的蒼蠅，
但蒼蠅總是很快又叮上她。
愛歐東奔西跑，
跳進海中，游到對岸。

但蒼蠅還是繼續叮咬她的頭和身體。
愛歐走過平原，爬上山坡，
蒼蠅一路緊隨在後。

- **put a spell on**
  咒語；魔力
- **follow** [`fɑ:loʊ]
  跟隨；追隨
- **easily** [`i:zəli]
  容易地；輕易地
- **swam** [swæm] 游泳
  （swim的過去式）
- **side** [saɪd] 側面的
- **continue** [kən`tɪnju:] 繼續
- **across** [ə`krɔ:s]
  橫越；穿過
- **plain** [pleɪn]
- **climb** [klaɪm] 爬；攀登

- **ran after** [ræn `æftə(r)]
  在……之後追著（ran是
  run的過去式）

p. 22

宙斯看著赫拉懲罰愛歐，
對愛歐深感憐憫。
他請求妻子讓蒼蠅不要再去咬她，
並發誓自己再也不會與愛歐交往，
還承諾自己會當個好丈夫。
赫拉知道他是真心誠意的，
便將蒼蠅身上的魔咒解除，
讓蒼蠅不再追著愛歐叮咬。

- **felt pity for**
  [felt `pɪti fə(r)]
  為……覺得抱歉
- **beg** [beg] 求情；乞求
- **promise** [`prɑ:mɪs]
  保證；允諾
- **sincere** [sɪn`sɪə(r)]
  誠實的；誠懇的
- **take away**
  移去；減去
- **chase** [tʃeɪs] 追逐；追趕

p. 23

接著，
宙斯也將愛歐身上的魔咒解除，
讓她變回成一位年輕的少婦。
她慢慢地試著說出話來，
因爲她怕自己一開口，
又是「哞」的叫聲。
不過這次她聽到自己輕柔的聲音，
她很興奮，
邊唱著歌，邊跑回家裡去了。

從此之後，愛歐再也不想談戀愛。
除了父親之外，
她甚至不看別的男人。
她只願意在父親的田裡工作，
她永遠不會忘記赫拉的懲罰的。

- **turned into** [tɜ:rnd `intu]
  轉變成……
- **tried to** 試著去……
  （tried是try的過去式）
- **soft** [sɔ:ft]
  輕柔的；溫和的
- **voice** [vɔɪs] 說話聲
- **ran back** [ræn beɪk] 爬回
- **afterward** [`æftərwərd]
  後來
- **another** [ən`ʌðə(r)]
  另一個的；再一個的
- **other than** [`ʌðə(r) ðæn]
  ……以外的
- **forget** [fər`ɡet] 忘記

13

卡麗絲托

赫拉將卡麗絲托變成一隻黑熊！

p. 24

阿蒂蜜絲和卡麗絲托是摯友。
阿蒂蜜絲是狩獵女神。
卡麗絲托是森林仙女。
她倆喜愛狩獵，居住在森林裡。

- **best** [best] 最好的（good 好的；better較好的）
- **goddess** [ˋgɑːdɪs] 女神
- **hunt** [hʌnt] 打獵
- **nymph** [ˋnɪmf] 寧芙（居於山林水澤的仙女）
- **enjoy** [ɪnˋdʒɔɪ] 享受；喜歡

---

p. 25

阿蒂蜜絲對卡麗絲托說：
「妳得答應我，永遠不要結婚。
妳結婚了，就會去住在城裡，
到時候妳會忘了我的。
沒有妳，我會很孤單。」
卡麗絲托回答：
「別擔心，我對男人沒有興趣，
我只想和妳住在森林裡。
我發誓我永遠不會結婚。」

- **promise** [ˋprɑːmɪs] 保證；允諾
- **run off** [rʌn ɔːf] 出走；逃走；離開
- **lonely** [ˋlounli] 孤單地
- **without** [wɪˋðaut] 無；缺
- **have no interest in** 對……沒有興趣
- **care about** [ker ˋəbaut] 在乎；關心
- **forest** [ˋfɔːrɪst] 森林

14

p. 26

一日，宙斯看見狩獵中的卡麗絲托，
便自言自語道：
「我得認識這女孩，
這女孩眞是絕美呀！」
但宙斯知道
卡麗絲托只喜歡阿蒂蜜絲，
便又心想：
「我得讓自己變成阿蒂蜜絲，
這樣卡麗絲托才不會對我起戒心。」
宙斯便先把自己
變成阿蒂蜜絲的樣子，
然後來到卡麗絲托的跟前。

- **make myself look like**
  使自己看起來像
- **trust** [trʌst] 相信；信任
- **appearance** [əˈpɪrəns]
  外貌；外表

p. 27

「原來妳在這裡呀，」
宙斯說：「跟我來一起享用午餐吧，
我找到了一些美味的葡萄。」
卡麗絲托開心地吃著葡萄，
她不知道宙斯已在葡萄裡下了魔咒。
只要吃下葡萄，
卡麗絲托便會愛上
她見到的第一個男人或是神。
宙斯看著卡麗絲托吃下第一顆葡萄。

- **found** [faʊnd]
  找到；發現（find的過
  去式）
- **lovely** [ˈlʌvli] 美好的
- **grape** [greɪp] 葡萄
- **gladly** [ˈɡlædli]
  高興地；愉快地
- **ate** [eɪt] 吃
  （eat的過去式）

15

p. 28

突然，宙斯變回他原來的模樣。
魔咒開始生效。
卡麗絲托愛上了宙斯，
成了他的情婦。
〔圖〕卡麗絲托和宙斯

卡麗絲托現在變得
沒有時間理會阿蒂蜜絲，
阿蒂蜜絲因此怨恨卡麗絲托，
決心永遠不再跟她說話。

- **original** [ə`rɪdʒənl]
  原始的；最初的
- **work** [wɜːrk]
  產生作用了
- **decide** [dɪ`saɪd] 決定
- **again** [ə`geɪn]
  再一次；復

---

p. 29

宙斯無法一直陪伴卡麗絲托，
他來一陣子之後便得離開，
讓卡麗絲托獨處數日或數週。
宙斯不在的時候，
卡麗絲托就很孤單。

有一天，卡麗絲托生下了一名男嬰。
「現在，我再也不孤單了。」
她心想：「你真是個漂亮的嬰兒！
而且長得很像你的爸爸宙斯，
我就把你取名做阿卡斯吧。」

- **spend . . . with**
  [spend wɪð]
  花費（時間）在……
- **left** [left] 丟下；遺忘
  （leave的過去式）
- **alone** [ə`loʊn] 單獨地
- **for days and weeks**
  歷經數日和數週
- **give birth to**
  [gɪv bɜːrθ tuː]
  生（孩子）；產下

p. 30

卡麗絲托教導阿卡斯
所有關於森林的所有知識。
一眨眼，
阿卡斯已經是個
又強壯又獨立的孩子了。
到了五歲時，
他的樣子看起來幾乎就和宙斯一樣。

這一天，赫拉在森林中散步。
當她看到阿卡斯時，她非常驚訝，
阿卡斯看起來是這麼面熟！

- **taught** [tɔːt] 教導；教授
  （teach的過去式）
- **everything** [ˈevriθiŋ]
  每一件事
- **independent**
  [ˌɪndɪˈpendənt] 獨立的
- **almost** [ˈɔːlmoust]
  幾乎；差不多
- **exactly** [ɪɡˈzæktli]
  正確地
- **through** [θruː] 穿越
- **familiar** [fəˈmɪliə(r)]
  熟悉的

p. 31

「這孩子和宙斯長得眞像，」
赫拉心中想著：
「宙斯到底做了什麼好事？」

赫拉非常氣憤，
她要阿卡斯帶她去見母親，
阿卡斯指著附近的卡麗絲托。
「讓我來教訓妳！」
赫拉斥責著卡麗絲托道：
「我要將妳
勾引我丈夫的美麗容貌奪走！」
不一會兒，
卡麗絲托看到自己的皮膚上
長出又黑又長的毛髮，
而且指甲變成了爪子。
卡麗絲托驚聲尖叫，
卻聽到自己發出一聲熊吼聲。
赫拉將卡麗絲托變成了一隻黑熊！

- **pointed at** 指著……
- **nearby** [ˈnɪrbaɪ]
  在附近的
- **beauty** [ˈbjuːti] 美貌
- **attract** [əˈtrækt]
  引起；吸引
- **in seconds** 轉眼間
- **skin** [skɪn] 皮膚
- **fingernail** [ˈfɪŋɡərneɪl]
  手指甲
- **claw** [klɔː] 爪子
- **roar** [rɔː(r)] 吼叫

p. 32

卡麗絲托跑向兒子阿卡斯，
但阿卡斯認不出她是母親，
還以為這隻黑熊要攻擊他！
阿卡斯轉身就跑，躲著自己的母親，
不知道母親發生了什麼事情。

他花了幾年的時間，
自己一個人孤伶伶地
在森林中尋找母親的身影。
還好他知道如何在森林求生存，
如今，
他已經是一位強壯的年輕男子了。

- **recognize** [`rekəgnaɪz]
  認出；看出
- **attack** [ə`tæk] 攻擊
- **turn** [tɜ:rn]
  轉過身去；別過臉去
- **ran away** 跑開（ran是
  run的過去式）
- **happen** [`hæpən] 發生
- **spent** [spent] 花費（時間）
  （spend的過去式）
- **look for** [lʊk fər]
  尋找；期待
- **grew up** 生長；長大
  （grew是grow的過去式）

p. 33

卡麗絲托也在森林中遊蕩，
找尋兒子。
日復一日，她越來越孤單，
對自己的處境難過不已。
她失去了摯友、情人，
最後連兒子也失去了。
人生是殘酷的，
她經常哭泣，
她的哭聲聽起來，
就好像她是一隻受了驚嚇的大熊。

有一天，卡麗絲托看到兒子在打獵，
她非常興奮，想和兒子打招呼。
她站起身子來，
但阿卡斯一看到她，
便舉起矛箭，準備殺了熊。

- **wander** [ˋwɑːndə(r)] 漫遊
- **lonelier** [ˋlounliər]
  更孤單的（lonely孤單的
  ，loneliest最孤單的）
- **lost** [lɔːst]
- **finally** [ˋfaɪnəli] 失去
- **seem** [siːm] 最終；最後
- **cruel** [kruːəl] 殘忍的
- **sound** [saund]
  聽起來……
- **scary** [ˋskeri] 易驚嚇的
- **hunt** [hʌnt] 打獵；狩獵
- **greet** [griːt]
  打招呼；歡迎
- **stood up** [stud ʌp]
  站起來（stood是stand的
  過去式）
- **hind legs** [haɪnd legz]
  後腳
- **picked up** [pɪkt ʌp]
  拾起；撿起
- **spear** [spɪr] 矛

20

p. 34

還好，宙斯看著這一切；
他知道這隻熊是卡麗絲托，
他認出阿卡斯是自己的兒子，
宙斯不希望有任何悲劇發生。

突然，宙斯抓起阿卡斯和卡麗絲托，
將兩人丟到天際成為星辰。
卡麗絲托成為大熊星座，
而阿卡斯成為小熊星座。
時至今日，
他們仍舊在天際閃閃發亮。

- **luckily** [ˋlʌkɪlɪ] 幸運地
- **recognize** [ˋrɛkəgnaɪz] 認出
- **terrible** [ˋtɛrəbl] 可怕的；駭人的
- **grab** [græb] 抓
- **threw** [θru] 丟
- **the Great Bear** 大熊星座
- **the Little Bear** 小熊星座
- **are shining** 正閃耀中
- **among** [əˋmʌŋ] 在……之中

達妮

宙斯一次次到來，
變成雨水淋在達妮身上。

p. 35

阿克里修斯是阿哥斯城的國王，
他的女兒達妮
是一位美麗的年輕公主，
但是，阿克里修斯並不快樂。
他希望能有個兒子，
將來在他死後，能夠繼承王位。

- **princess** [ˋprɪnses] 公主
- **daughter** [ˋdɔːtə(r)] 女兒
- **son** [sʌn] 兒子
- **become** [bɪˋkʌm] 成為
- **die** [daɪ] 死去

---

p. 36

阿克里修斯來到狄菲神殿，
求取神諭。
他問道：「神諭，
請告訴我如何能夠有個兒子，
我逐漸老去，需要有人在我死後，
繼承王位。」
神諭卻告訴阿克里修斯一個壞消息：
「你將永遠不會有兒子。
而且，令嬡會生個孫子，
孫子將來會殺了你。」
阿克里修斯的臉色頓時變得慘白。
自己的親人竟然會殺了他！

- **oracle** [ˋɔːrəkl]
  先知；神諭
- **Delphi** [ˋdɛlfaɪ] 狄菲神殿
- **need** [niːd] 需要
- **someone** [ˋsʌmwʌn] 某人
- **grandson** [ˋgrændsʌn]
  孫子
- **grew white** [gru waɪt]
  （臉色）轉白
- **a member of**
  [ə ˋmembə(r) ɑːv]
  ……的一員

p. 37

阿克里修斯非常害怕死亡，
更不希望死在自己孫子的手裡！
「我知道非這麼做不可，」
他心想：
「我決不能讓達妮懷孕生子，
只要她不生小孩，我便不會被殺。」
阿克里修斯召喚僕役前來。
「我要你們將達妮關進監牢，
絕對不可以把她放出來！」

- be afraid of
  [bi ə`freɪd ɑ:v] 害怕……
- death [deθ] 死亡
- hate [heɪt] 憎恨；厭惡
- give birth [gɪv bɜ:rθ]
  生（孩子）；產下
- servant [`sɜ:rvənt]
  侍從；僕人
- prison [`prɪzn] 監牢

p. 38

僕人抓著達妮，將她關進監牢。
達妮一路上大聲尖叫道：
「你們為什麼要這麼做？
我做錯了什麼事情，
要受這樣的處罰？」

達妮在監獄中度過多年光陰，
這裡不見天日，
沒有人可以講話，
讓她變得非常憂傷寂寞。

- deserve [dɪ`zɜ:rv]
  應受（賞罰）
- never [`nevə(r)]
  再不會；不可能
- daylight [`deɪlaɪt]
  日光；白晝光
- person [`pɜ:rsn] 人

23

p. 39

但宙斯可以看到達妮，
他可以看到地面上、
地底下的一切事情。
他心想：「美人是不該孤單的，
我要成為她的朋友。」
但宙斯又憂心道：
「如果我穿過牆壁去看她，
一定會嚇到她的，
不如我就變成金黃色的雨水，
淋在她身上，讓她快樂！」

- **over** [ˈouvə(r)] 遍及……
- **on** [ɑ:n] 在……之上
- **below** [bɪˈlou]
  在…… 之下
- **worried** [ˈwɜ:rid] 煩惱的
- **wall** [wɔ:l] 牆
- **instead** [ɪnˈsted]
  取而代之的
- **golden rain**
  [ˈgouldən reɪn] 黃金雨
- **pour down** [pɔ:r daun]
  傾盆而下

p. 40

〔圖〕金黃雨水淋在達妮身上
當達妮抬頭望著屋頂，
她看到金黃色的雨水降下，
雨水乾淨而美麗。

- **ceiling** [ˈsi:lɪŋ] 天花板
- **falling** [ˈfɔ:lɪŋ]
  落下的；降下的
- **golden** [ˈgouldən]
  黃金色的

p. 41

進了牢裡以後，
達妮第一次覺得快樂。
讓她忘掉了所有的痛苦。
宙斯一次次到來，
變成雨水淋在達妮身上。

有一天，
雨水淋在她身上淋了好幾個小時。
金黃雨水穿過她的皮膚，
雨水裡有宙斯的種。

達妮懷孕了，
她的肚子大了起來。
侍衛發現達妮的大肚子，
便稟告國王阿克里修斯：
「啊，國王陛下，
公主即將臨盆了！」
阿克里修斯憤怒不已，斥道：
「怎麼會這樣？
一定是你讓男人進去看她！
你們這些侍衛都要接受處罰！」
所有侍衛均被處決。
新的侍衛繼續看守監獄，
達妮仍舊被囚禁在獄中。

- **problem** [ˈprɑːbləm] 疑問；難題
- **again and again** [əˈɡeɪn ənd əˈɡeɪn] 一次又一次地
- **rain upon** [reɪn əˈpɑːn] 落在……之上
- **seed** [siːd] 種子
- **pregnant** [ˈpreɡnənt] 懷孕的
- **stomach** [ˈstʌmək] 胃
- **guard** [ɡɑːrd] 護衛
- **notice** [ˈnoʊtɪs] 注意；察覺
- **scream** [skriːm] 驚呼；尖叫
- **allow** [əˈlaʊ] 允許
- **visit** [ˈvɪzɪt] 探訪
- **punish** [ˈpʌnɪʃ] 懲罰
- **remain** [rɪˈmeɪn] 仍是；保持不變
- **locked** [lɑːkt] 被鎖著
- **cell** [sel] 單身牢房

25

p. 42

終於，達妮生了一個兒子。
她為兒子取名為「柏修斯」。
國王下令將達妮和柏修斯帶來見他。
「這就是有朝一日會殺死我的孫子？」
他說：
「我絕不容許這種事情發生！
來人！將他們裝進木箱，
把箱子丟入大海中！」

- **named** [neɪmd] 命名為
- **brought** [brɔt] 帶來
- **permit** [pə`mɪt] 允許；容許
- **put . . . in** [pʊt ɪn] 放……進入……
- **wooden** [`wʊdn] 木製的；木造的
- **throw into** 丟進……

p. 43

侍衛依令照辦，
但是箱子並沒有沈沒，
而是浮在水面上。
箱子被海浪帶到遙遠的地方。
達妮和柏修斯沒有食物和水。
過了許久，箱子漂到瑟律弗島；
島上的國王是迪克提士，
他看著箱子從遠處漂來，
「將箱子取過來！」他對僕役說。

- **order** [`ɔ:rdər] 命令；指示
- **sink** [sɪŋk] 沉沒；沉入
- **float on** [floʊt ɑ:n] 在……漂浮
- **far away** [fɑ:(r) ə`weɪ] 遠遠地
- **wave** [weɪv] 波浪；海浪
- **the island of Serifos** 瑟律弗島
- **servant** [`sɜ:rvənt] 侍從；僕人

26

p. 44

「讓我看看裡面有什麼東西。」
迪克提士國王
看著裡頭的達妮和柏修斯，
十分驚訝。
「請給我們食物和水吧。」達妮說。
迪克提士國王是個好人，
他爲他們準備食物和水，
並下令僕人服侍這對母子。
沒多久，
達妮和柏修斯恢復了健康和體力。

- **inside** [`ɪn`saɪd]
  在內部的
- **shocked** [ʃɑ:kd] 震驚的
- **kind** [kaɪnd]
  親切的；友好的
- **gave** [geɪv] 給予；捐助
  （give的過去式）
- **healthy** [`helθi]
  健康地；健全地

p. 45

達妮告訴迪克提士國王
他們母子的遭遇，
國王對於阿克里修斯的行徑，
感到驚駭。
一個男人
如何能對自己的親人如此殘酷？

迪克提士愛上了達妮。
她是個堅強的女人，
也是一位好母親。
她保護柏修斯，
讓他得以存活。
達妮有著皇后般的美貌和優雅氣質，
因此迪克提士娶了達妮。

柏修斯長大之後，
成爲一位健壯的年輕人。
他有許多冒險經歷。
在一次冒險活動中，
他遇到阿克里修斯，並且殺了他。
接著他成爲阿哥斯城的國王，
這原是阿克里修斯的王國。

- **horrify** [ˋhɔːrɪfaɪ]
  使毛骨悚然；使恐懼
- **behavior** [bɪˋheɪvjə(r)]
  行爲；舉止
- **protect** [prəˋtekt] 保護
- **alive** [əˋlaɪv]
  活著的；充滿生氣的
- **charm** [tʃɑːrm] 魅力
- **marry** [ˋmæri] 結婚
- **adventure** [ədˋventʃə(r)]
  冒險

愛克美娜

宙斯希望
能與愛克美娜單獨在一起。

p. 46

愛克美娜也是宙斯的情婦。
當然,她非常美麗,
許多男士紛紛為她著迷,
但她卻嫁給平庸的安菲屈昂。
安菲屈昂能夠娶到愛克美娜,
大家都說是他的福氣。

- **be attracted to**
  [bi ə`træktɪd tə]
  被……吸引
- **ordinary** [`ɔ:rdneri]
  普通的
- **thought** [θɔ:t] 想;認為
  (think的過去式)
- **lucky** [`lʌki]
  幸運的;僥倖的

p. 47

但是安菲屈昂的好運沒能維持多久,
因為宙斯對愛克美娜一見鍾情。
宙斯希望能與愛克美娜單獨在一起。
但這並不容易,
因為她已經嫁作人婦,
常與丈夫形影不離。
宙斯得想個辦法。

- **luck** [lʌk] 運氣
- **last** [læst]
- **soon** [su:n]
  不久;沒一會兒工夫
- **at first sight**
  一眼(就)……
- **difficult** [`dɪfɪkəlt]
  困難的;不容易的
- **make a plan**
  [meɪk ə plæn]
  想個辦法;擬訂計畫

p. 48

幾天之後，
愛克美娜得到不幸的消息。
她的兄弟們被殺了！
消息如下：

有位年老的牧羊人，
撞見她的兄弟們想偷羊隻，
老牧羊人把他們趕走，
他知道他們還會再回來，
便把自己的四個兒子叫到田原上，
躲起來等他們回來，
待他們一來，就一舉殺了他們。

- **shepherd** [ˈʃepərd]
  牧羊人
- **steal** [stiːl] 偷盜
- **scare away** [skerəˈweɪ]
  嚇走
- **field** [fiːld] 田野；田原
- **hide** [haɪd] 躲藏；躲避
- **wait** [weɪt] 等；等候
- **return** [rɪˈtɜːrn]
  返回；歸回

p. 49

愛克美娜聽到消息，
並沒有哭泣，而是非常憤怒。
「我的兄弟們為什麼要接受
如此殘酷的懲罰？
他們的罪行又不重，
只需坐牢，不該為此喪命的。」
愛克美娜告訴丈夫說：
「我要報復，殺人犯是老牧羊人，
他住在島上的另一邊，請你殺了他。」
但安菲屈昂並不想照辦。

- **heard** [hɜːrd]
  聽聞（hear的過去式）
- **badly** [ˋbædli]
  嚴重地；極端地
- **crime** [kraɪm] 罪行
- **serious** [ˋsɪriəs]
  認真的；危及的
- **demand** [dɪˋmænd] 要求
- **revenge** [rɪˋvendʒ] 復仇

31

p. 50

愛克美娜一次次要求他殺了老牧羊人，
安菲屈昂不得安寧，
他知道妻子是永遠不會饒恕牧羊人的，
因此他來到島的另一邊。

他爬上他所知道最高的山峰，
接著尋找羊群。
他看到了一大群羊，
有位老人看管著羊。
安菲屈昂從山上下來，
躲在樹叢中，後來睡著了。

- **peace** [piːs] 講和；和平
- **forgive** [fərˋgɪv]
  原諒；寬恕
- **climb** [klaɪm] 爬；攀登
- **highest** [ˋhaɪghest] 最高
  的（high高的；higher較
  高的）
- **hill** [hɪl] 小山
- **flock** [flɑːk] 一群（同類
  牲畜尤指鴨、羊）
- **bush** [buʃ] 灌木矮樹

p. 51

夜晚時分，安菲屈昂醒來。
他來到老人之前所在的地方。

幾個小時過後，
他看到一名老人走來。
由於夜晚視線不佳，
安菲屈昂看不清楚老人的臉。
「這一定是那位老牧羊人了。」
安菲屈昂心想著。
待老人靠近的時候，
他便一躍而出，
將刀刺入老人的背部。
老人應聲而死。

- **woke up** [wok ʌp] 醒來
  （woke是wake的過去式）
- **until** [ənˋtɪl] 直到……時
- **close** [klous] 接近地
- **jump up** 一躍而起
- **push into** [puʃ ɪntə]
  刺入；戳入
- **knife** [naɪf]
  （有柄的）小刀

p. 52

安菲屈昂回到家中，
卻發現妻子在哭泣。
「愛克美娜，妳為什麼哭泣呢？」
他問道。
「噢！有人殺了父親。」
愛克美娜哭著說道：
「父親在深夜裡步行回家，
一定有人誤認他是個賊！」
愛克美娜搗著臉哭泣。
「這真是悲慘啊！」
她哭著說：「短短一週內，
我便失去了兄弟和父親！
這叫我如何能承受！」

- **late at night**
  [leɪt ət naɪt] 深夜
- **thief** [θiːf] 小偷；盜賊
- **held . . . in** [held ɪn]
  捧著……在……
  （held是hold的過去式）
- **terrible** [ˋterəbl]
  駭人的；可怕的
- **lost** [lɔːst] 失掉；失去
  （lose的過去式）
- **stand** [stænd]
  忍受；抵抗

p. 53

安菲屈昂這才發現
自己誤殺了岳父大人，
他心中難過不已，
決定告訴妻子實情。
他說：「愛妻，請妳原諒我，
是我殺了岳父的，
我以為他是那位老牧羊人。
請妳原諒我！」
愛克美娜跪倒在地，說到：
「還有什麼比這個更悽慘的！
這種事怎麼會發生啊！」

- **realize** [ˋrɪəlaɪz]
  認知到；體悟
- **decide** [dɪsˋaɪd] 決定
- **truth** [truːθ] 真相；事實
- **forgive** [fərˋgɪv] 原諒
- **floor** [flɔː(r)] 地板
- **worst** [wɜːst] 最糟的；
  最壞的（bad糟的；
  worse較糟的）
- **happen** [ˋhæpən] 發生
- **true** [truː]
  真實的；確實的

35

p. 54

安菲屈昂走到外面，
街上有許多人。
他大聲喊道：
「我殺了自己的岳父，
我必須爲自己的錯付出代價，
請各位決定我該接受什麼樣的懲罰。」

城裡的人舉行會議，
他們討論著應該如何處罰安菲屈昂。
最後，
他們決定將他送到附近的一個小島。
那是一個無人之島，
在那裡，安菲屈昂將無法傷害任何人。

- **walk** [wɔ:k] 步行；行走
- **outside** [ˋaʊtˋsaɪd] 屋外的
- **street** [stri:t] 街道
- **shout** [ʃaʊt] 大叫；叫喊
- **pay for** [peɪ fə(r)] 爲……付出代價
- **mistake** [mɪsˋteɪk] 錯誤
- **townspeople** [ˋtaʊnzpi:pl] 鎮上居民
- **meeting** [ˋmi:tɪŋ] 會議
- **argue about** [ˋɑ:rgju: əˋbaʊt] 爭論……；爭吵……
- **nearby** [ˋnɪrbaɪ] 在附近的
- **anyone** [ˋeniwʌn] 任何人

p. 55

愛克美娜又哭了起來，
她對於丈夫殺父感到憤怒，
但她了解這是個無心之過：
「我必須原諒我的丈夫。」
她告訴城裡的人說：
「我們結婚時，
我許諾過永遠與他同在，
我願隨他去無人島。」
於是，兩人便離開城鎮。

安菲屈昂很高興有妻子隨行，
但妻子仍舊對他心有怒氣。

- **began** [bɪˋgæn] 開始
  （begin 的過去式）
- **kill** [kɪl] 殺死
- **agreed to** [əˋgriːd tuː]
  同意於
- **stay with** [steɪ wɪð]
  同……在一起
- **go with** [gou wɪð]
  與……前往
- **left** [left]
  離開（leave 的過去式）
- **forever** [fərˋevə(r)]
  永遠的
- **still** [stɪl] 仍然；依舊

p. 56

在小島上的第一天，
愛克美娜對安菲屈昂說：
「我仍舊希望為兄弟報仇，
除非你殺了牧羊人，
否則我是不會和你說話的。」

安菲屈昂因為妻子不與他說話，
感到悶悶不樂。
最後，他再也無法忍受，
便帶著武器，離開這小島。

- **revenge** [ˈrɪvendʒ] 復仇
- **until** [ənˈtɪl] 直到……時
- **stand** [stænd] 忍受
- **longer** [ˈlɔːŋgə(r)]
  更長的（時間）
- **pack** [pæk] 打包；捆紮
- **weapon** [ˈwepən] 武器

p. 57

因為安菲屈昂是不應該去牧羊人所在的
島上的，
所以他必須非常小心。
他只在晚間行事，
並睡在山裡頭。

他走得很慢，
不希望有人看見他。
他已經離開妻子數個月了，
他開始想念愛克美娜。

- **was not supposed to**
  不應該是……
- **careful** [ˈkɛrfəl]
  小心的；當心的
- **travel** [ˈtrævl] 遊歷
- **slept** [slɛpt]
  睡覺（sleep的過去式）
- **slowly** [ˈseloʊlɪ] 緩慢的
- **several** [ˈsvrəl]
  幾個；一些
- **miss** [mɪs] 想念

p. 58

這對宙斯來說，是個良機。
事實上，這一切都是宙斯的詭計；
宙斯看著愛克美娜的兄弟們被殺，
讓愛克美娜心生報復之心，
並讓城民將安菲屈昂遣送到無人島上。

現在，宙斯可以和愛克美娜單獨相處了，
他的計畫非常成功。
宙斯飛到小島上，改變容貌，
將自己變成安菲屈昂的模樣。

- **perfect** [ˋpɜːrfɪkt]
  完美的；絕佳的
- **chance** [tʃæns] 機會
- **create** [kriˋeɪt] 創造
- **entire** [ɪnˋtaɪə(r)] 完整的
- **situation** [ˏsɪtʃuˋeɪʃən]
  情況
- **make sure** [meɪk ʃʊr]
  確定
- **cause** [kɔːz]
  引起；使遭受

p. 59

宙斯來到愛克美娜面前，
對她說：「我回來了，愛妻，
我已經殺了老牧羊人。
妳的仇已經報了。」
愛克美娜放下手邊的籃子，
跑到宙斯面前，對他又親又抱。
「親愛的安菲屈昂！
你聽從我的話！
你是真心愛我的！
現在我也可以全心愛你了。」
愛克美娜並不知道，
眼前的這個人其實是宙斯。

- **drop** [drɑ:p] 丟
- **basket** [bɪskɪt] 籃子
- **hug** [hʌg] 擁抱；摟
- **dearest** [dɪrɪst]
  最親愛的
- **with all my heart**
  全心全意
- **actually** [ˈæktʃuəli]
  事實上；實際上

41

p. 60

一日，
宙斯知道安菲屈昂即將返回島上。
因此便在他們夫妻相見之前離開。

安菲屈昂來到愛克美娜面前，
跪了下來。
「我感到非常抱歉，
親愛的愛克美娜，
我無法下手殺牧羊人，
當我看到他蒼老的面容，
我就心生憐憫，下不了手了，
請妳原諒我！」

- **come back** [kʌm bæk]
  回來
- **bent down** [bent daʊn]
  彎下（bent是bend的過去式）
- **on one's knee**
  在某人的膝蓋上
- **dear** [dɪr] 親愛的
- **was not able to**
  沒辦法
- **forgive** [fərˋgɪv]
  原諒；寬恕

p. 61

愛克美娜感到困惑。
「你在說什麼？八個月前，
你就說你已經殺了他了！」
進來吧，親愛的，我想你是中暑了。」
安菲屈昂不知道發生了什麼事。

他不知道愛克美娜那天是在說什麼，
但他決心不再提起此事。
同樣地，
愛克美娜也不知道宙斯曾和她相愛過。

對於安菲屈昂來說，
愛妻是世上最寬容的人；
對愛克美娜來說，
丈夫則是最偉大的英雄了。

- **confused** [kən`fju:zd]
  疑惑的
- **talk about** [tɔ:k ə`baʊt]
  談論關於
- **meant** [ment] 意指
  （mean的過去式）
- **greatest** [`greɪtɪst] 最棒的
  （great棒的；greater較棒
  的）
- **hero** [`hɪroʊ] 英雄
- **ever** [`evə(r)] 曾經

43

閱讀測驗

※ 閱讀下列問題並選出最適當的答案。 ➜ 62-65 頁

●愛歐

1. 宙斯把愛歐變成了什麼？

    (A) 一頭野獸。

    (B) 一位女神。

    (C) 一個禮物。

    (D) 一頭母牛。

                                答案 (D)

2. 為什麼愛歐無法對他的家人說話？

    (A) 因為她只能發出「哞」的聲音。

    (B) 因為她總是在吃東西。

    (C) 因為她已經變成一隻蒼蠅。

    (D) 因為她哭得太傷心而無法說話。

                                答案 (A)

3. 赫拉是如何懲罰愛歐的？

    (A) 她把愛歐的眼睛從她頭上取下來。

    (B) 她遣了一隻蒼蠅去咬愛歐。

    (C) 她把愛歐的眼睛拿來裝飾孔雀。

    (D) 她打愛歐的頭。

                                答案 (B)

●卡麗絲托

4. 神奇的葡萄對卡麗絲托產生了什麼作用？

    (A) 使她愛上阿蒂蜜絲。

    (B) 使她對男人失去興趣。

    (C) 使她憎恨阿蒂蜜絲。

    (D) 使她愛上宙斯。　　　　答案 (D)

5. 赫拉對卡麗絲托做了什麼？

    (A) 她把卡麗絲托變成一隻熊。

    (B) 她把卡麗絲托變成一個強壯的男子。

    (C) 她把卡麗絲托變成一個星座。

    (D) 她大聲斥責卡麗絲托。　　答案 (A)

6. 宙斯如何防止阿卡斯殺死自己的母親？

    (A) 他把他們變消失了。

    (B) 他把阿卡斯的矛拿走。

    (C) 他把阿卡斯和卡麗絲托變成天上的星星
       了。

    (D) 他叫阿卡斯不要這麼做。　答案 (C)

46

7. 為什麼阿克里修斯想要一個兒子?

(A) 因為他討厭女兒。

(B) 因為他希望死後能有個兒子來繼續王位。

(C) 因為他的兒子比女兒強壯。

(D) 因為他是個懦夫。

答案 (B)

8. 為什麼阿克里修斯要把達妮關在牢獄中?

(A) 如此一來她將不可能懷孕生孩子。

(B) 因為他討厭他女兒。

(C) 如此一來她將無法殺害阿克里修斯。

(D) 因為這對她的健康很好。

答案 (A)

9. 當守衛把箱子丟近海裡之後,發生了什麼事?

(A) 箱子沉下去了。

(B) 箱子破掉了。

(C) 箱子彈了一下。

(D) 箱子浮在海上。

答案 (D)

10. 爲什麼說安菲屈昂是一個幸運的男人？

(A) 因爲他貴爲國王。

(B) 因爲他娶了一位美嬌娘。

(C) 因爲他家財萬貫。

(D) 因爲他貌若潘安。

答案 (B)

11. 爲什麼愛克美娜的父親會被殺？

(A) 因爲安菲屈昂把他誤認爲老牧羊人。

(B) 因爲愛克美娜偷了羊。

(C) 因爲安菲屈昂是個邪惡的人。

(D) 因爲愛克美娜的父親是個老人。

答案 (A)

12. 爲什麼宙斯要愛克美娜的哥哥們被殺？

(A) 因爲他討厭他們。

(B) 因爲他喜歡傷心的故事。

(C) 因爲他喜歡捉弄愛克美娜。

(D) 因爲他想要跟愛克美娜單獨在一起。

答案 (D)

※閱讀下段文章，並討論之以下的問題。 ➔ 66-67 頁

……從此之後，愛歐再也不想談戀愛。除了父親之外，她甚至不看別的男人。她只願意在父親的田裡工作，她永遠不會忘記赫拉的懲罰的。

1. 「她永遠不會忘記赫拉的懲罰。」這句話是什麼意思？
   如果你是愛歐，你會怎麼做？

參考答案

It means that Io would never forget how Hera punished her for being Zeus's lover.

I would be more careful about falling in love with a god.

這表示愛歐永遠不會忘記當宙斯的愛人是如何受到赫拉的懲罰。

我會在與神談戀愛時更加小心。

……有一天，卡麗絲托看到兒子在打獵，她非常興奮，想和兒子打招呼。她站起身子來，但阿卡斯一看到她，便舉起矛箭，準備殺了熊。……

2. 在這種情況下，如果你是卡麗絲托，你會怎麼做？

參考答案

I would not act fierce. Instead, I would act strangely so that Arcas would become curious about me.

我不會表現得兇猛，而是會作一些奇怪的動作，好讓他覺得古怪。

……「我知道非這麼做不可，」他心想：「我決不能讓達妮懷孕生子，只要她不生小孩，我便不會被殺。」

阿克里修斯召喚僕役前來。「我要你們將達妮關進監牢，絕對不可以把她放出來！」……

3. 阿克里修斯把達妮關進牢獄，難道沒有其他方法能解決女兒的問題嗎？如果你是阿克里修斯，你會怎麼做？

[參考答案]

I would have told Danae exactly what the oracle told me.

我會將神諭所說的，一五一十地告訴他。

……由於夜晚視線不佳，安菲屈昂看不清楚老人的臉。「這一定是那位老牧羊人了。」安菲屈昂心想著。

待老人靠近的時候，他便一躍而出，將刀刺入老人的背部。老人應聲而死。……

4. 安菲屈昂以為愛克美娜的父親就是那個老牧羊人，在這種情況下，如果你是安菲屈昂，你會怎麼做？

[參考答案]

I would have followed the old man to make sure he was the old shepherd before killing him.

我會在下手之前，先確認他就是那個老牧羊人。

黃道十二宮

黃道十二宮　→ 68~72 頁

「黃道帶」（zodiac）這個字源自希臘文，意指「動物的環狀軌道」。黃道帶的起源為何？在本篇裡，你將可以看到說明星座來源的希臘神話故事：

太陽（the Sun）、地球（the Earth）、牡羊座（the Ram）、金牛座（the Bull）、雙子座（the Twins）、巨蟹座（the Crab）、獅子座（the Lion）、處女座（the Virgin）、天秤座（the Balance）、天蠍座（the Scorpion）、射手座（the Archer）、摩羯座（the Goat）、寶瓶座（the Water Bearer）、雙魚座（the Fishes）。

1. Aries（the Ram）牡羊座
2. Libra（the Balance）天秤座
3. Taurus（the Bull）金牛座
4. Scorpio（the Scorpion）天蠍座
5. Gemini（the Twins）雙子座
6. Sagittarius（the Archer）射手座
7. Cancer（the Crab）巨蟹座
8. Capricorn（the Goat）摩羯座
9. Leo（The Lion）獅子座
10. Aquarius（the Water Bearer）寶瓶座
11. Virgo（the Virgin）處女座
12. Pisces（the Fishes）雙魚座

牡羊座（the Ram）　3.21-4.20

牡羊座源自於金羊毛的故事。白羊安全營救福里瑟斯，福里瑟斯把金羊獻祭給宙斯作為回報，宙斯便將金羊形象化為天上星座。

金牛座（the Bull）　4.21-5.20

金牛座源自於歐羅巴和公牛的故事。宙斯化身為公牛，以便吸引歐羅巴，公牛載著歐羅巴跨海來到克里特島。宙斯將公牛的形象化為星座，以為紀念。

雙子座（the Twins）　5.21-6.21

雙子座源自於卡斯特與波樂克斯的故事。他們兩人為孿生兄弟，彼此相親相愛。為了紀念其兄弟情誼，宙斯將他們的形象化為星座。

巨蟹座（the Crab）　6.22-7.22

巨蟹座源自於赫丘力的十二項苦差役。希拉派遣巨蟹前去殺害赫丘力，但是赫丘力在打敗九頭蛇之前，一腳將巨蟹踩碎。為了紀念巨蟹，希拉將其形象化為星座。

獅子座（The Lion）　7.23-8.22

獅子座亦源自於赫丘力十二項苦差中。赫丘力的第一項苦差，是要殺死奈米亞山谷之獅。他徒手殺了獅子，為了紀念這項偉大的事蹟，宙斯將奈米亞獅子的形象，置於星辰之中。

處女座（the Virgin）　8.23-9.22

處女座源自於潘朵拉的故事。處女指的是純潔與天真女神阿絲蒂雅。潘朵拉好奇將禁盒打開，讓許多邪惡事物來到人間，眾神紛紛返回天庭。為了紀念這種失落的純真，便把阿絲蒂雅的形象置於群星中。

天秤座（the Balance） 9.23-10.21

天秤是正義的秤子，由神聖正義女神蒂米絲隨身攜帶。天秤座落在處女座旁邊，因為阿絲蒂雅是蒂米絲之女。

天蠍座（the Scorpion） 10.22-11.21

天蠍座源自於歐里昂。歐里昂和阿蒂蜜絲是一對狩獵夥伴，阿蒂蜜絲的哥哥阿波羅對此忌妒不已。他請求蓋亞殺了歐里昂。因此，蓋亞創造天蠍殺了偉大的歐里昂。為了紀念此事，宙斯將歐里昂和天蠍化成星座。這兩個星座從來不會同時出現。

射手座（the Archer） 11.23-12.21

射手座代表卡隆。在希臘神話故事中，卡隆是許多英雄的朋友，例如亞吉力、赫丘力。赫丘力以毒箭誤傷了卡隆。卡隆是神，因此得以不死，但是卻必須忍受這無止盡的痛苦，所以卡隆央求宙斯殺了他。為了紀念卡隆，宙斯將他化為星座。

摩羯座（the Goat） 12.22-1.19

魔羯代表哺育年幼宙斯的羊阿瑪爾夏。
據說宙斯為了感念此羊，將之化為星座。

寶瓶座（the Water Bearer） 1.20-2.18

寶瓶座源自於鐸卡連的洪水。在這個故事中，宙
斯在人間降下豪雨，讓洪水沖走一切邪惡的生
物。只有鐸卡連和妻子皮雅是洪水的生還者。

雙魚座（the Fishes） 2.19-3.20

雙魚座代表愛與美之女神阿芙柔黛蒂，
以及其子愛神愛羅斯。當時有個颱風，
兩人沿著優芙瑞特河步行。他們請求宙
斯援救，宙斯將兩人變成魚，讓他們安
然渡過風災。為了紀念此事，阿芙柔黛
蒂化身為星座中的大魚，愛羅斯則化為
小魚。

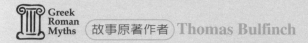

Without a knowledge of mythology much of the elegant literature of our own language cannot be understood and appreciated.

　　缺少了神話知識，就無法了解和透徹語言的文學之美。

—*Thomas Bulfinch*

　　Thomas Bulfinch（1796-1867），出生於美國麻薩諸塞州的Newton，隨後全家移居波士頓，父親為知名的建築師Charles Bulfinch。他在求學時期，曾就讀過一些優異的名校，並於1814年畢業於哈佛。

　　畢業後，執過教鞭，爾後從商，但經濟狀況一直未能穩定。1837年，在銀行擔任一般職員，以此為終身職業。後來開始進一步鑽研古典文學，成為業餘作家，一生未婚。

　　1855年，時值59歲，出版了奠立其作家地位的名作*The Age of Fables*，書中蒐集希臘羅馬神話，廣受歡迎。此書後來與日後出版的 *The Age of Chivalry*（1858）和 *Legends of Charlemagne*（1863），合集更名為 *Bulfinch's Mythology*。

　　本系列書系，即改編自 *The Age of Fable*。Bulfinch 著寫本書時，特地以成年大眾為對象，以將古典文學引介給一般大眾。*The Age of Fable* 堪稱十九世紀的羅馬神話故事的重要代表著作，其中有很多故事來源，來自Bulfinch自己對奧維德（Ovid）的《變形記》（*Metamorphoses*）的翻譯。

■Bulfinch 的著作

1. Hebrew Lyrical History.
2. The Age of Fable: Or Stories of Gods and Heroes.
3. The Age of Chivalry.
4. The Boy Inventor: A Memoir of Matthew Edwards, Mathematical-Instrument Maker.
5. Legends of Charlemagne.
6. Poetry of the Age of Fable.
7. Shakespeare Adapted for Reading Classes.
8. Oregon and Eldorado.
9. Bulfinch's Mythology: Age of Fable, Age of Chivalry, Legends of Charlemagne.